Christmas 1999

With love, from a

very special pen-friend

Mum & Dad

dEdicated to
all of
THE BABIES.

PENGUIN DREAMS

J. Otto Seibold and V. L. Walsh

chronicle books · san francisco

Shhhhhh...

Chongo Chingi is

**But even when
sleeping,
a penguin keeps
thinking.**

Chongo Chingi is

DREAMING

Thoughts are flying
round and round,
thoughts of flying
off the ground.

"Icicle-barnicle,
what shall we do?"

"We'll meet in the water!"
and off they flew.

One to the water,
one to the air...

Chongo didn't know he could go up there.

BEEP-BEEP

Space is no trouble...

...if you float like a bubble.

**Ring-aling-ling...
Ding-dong-dingi...
Time to wake-up
Chongo Chingi!**

Book design by J.otto Seibold.
Typeset in Honky and Rosewood.
The illustrations in this book were rendered on an
Apple computer Power Macintosh 8500/120. Using
Adobe Illustrator v6.0 software.
Printed in Hong Kong.

Library of Congress Cataloging-in-Publication Data
Seibold, J.otto.
Penguin dreams / J.otto Seibold and V.L. Walsh.
p. cm.
Summary: Chongo Chingi the penguin has a dream in
which he experiences the excitement of flying, but
then he must wake up.
ISBN 0-8118-2558-2
[1. Penguins Fiction. 2. Flight Fiction. 3. Stories in
rhyme.] I. Walsh, Vivian. II. Title.
PZ8.3.S457Pe   1999
[E]—dc21   99-16586
                            CIP

Distributed in Canada by Raincoast Books
8680 Cambie Street, Vancouver,
British Columbia V6P 6M9

10 9 8 7 6 5 4 3 2

Chronicle Books
85 Second Street, San Francisco, California 94105

www.chroniclebooks.com/Kids

beak

belly

eyes

flippers

boots

THE QUOTE THAT APPEARS ON THE BACK
COVER IS BY THEADORA WALSH

AGE 3
1995

orange

white

blue

black

tangerine